SEP 10 2015

Maisy's
Library
Card
02-10
1990

First published by Walker Books Ltd.,
87 Vauxhall Walk, London SE11 5HJ

Copyright © 2005 by Lucy Cousins
Lucy Cousins font copyright © 2005 by Lucy Cousins
Illustrated in the style of Lucy Cousins by King Rollo Films Ltd.

Maisy™. Maisy is a registered trademark of Walker Books Ltd., London.

First U.S. paperback edition 2009

Library of Congress Cataloging-in-Publication Data is available.

Library of Congress Catalog Card Number 2004051877

ISBN 978-0-7636-2669-3 (hardcover)
ISBN 978-0-7636-4371-3 (paperback)

14 15 16 SCP 10 9 8 7 6 5

Printed in Humen, Dongguan, China

This book was typeset in Lucy Cousins.
The illustrations were done in gouache.

Candlewick Press
99 Dover Street
Somerville, Massachusetts 02144

visit us at www.candlewick.com

Maisy Goes to the Library

Lucy Cousins

CANDLEWICK PRESS

Maisy likes going to the library.

She loves to read a book in a nice, quiet place.

Today, Maisy
wanted to read
a book about fish.

She found a blue
book about birds.

And she found an orange stripy book about tigers, but no fish.

So Maisy
kept looking.

There are
lots of other
things to do in
the library, too.

Use the
computer.

Listen
to music.

Make copies
of your
favorite
picture.

And look at
fish in the
aquarium.

Aquarium?

That's it! So Maisy looked by the aquarium.

That's where she found
a book about fish.
It was sparkly!

Maisy sat down to read her book in a quiet corner.

Then Cyril and Tallulah came along.

Tallulah made a funny face, and they started laughing!

Then Eddie came in.

"Story time!" he shouted.

"There was an old woman who swallowed a fly," Ostrich began.

charley started laughing.

"She swallowed a dog to catch the cat!" Ostrich read.

Now everyone was laughing!

Woof-woof!

They were still
laughing when they
checked out their books

and went outside
to play.

In the park, Cyril and Charley pretended to be the old woman and her dog.

Tallulah meowed like a cat, and
Eddie neighed like a horse.

Meow!

Neigh!

And Maisy read her sparkly book about fish in a nice, quiet place.